Dedicated to those that get it....

Pandora's Jar

by Ian Phillips

The jar stood, as it always had, on the second shelf. Not the uppermost.
That was reserved for the antiquities as George described them. Ancient
instruments of the trade. He had insisted on that. Let's remind customers
how far medicine has come. He had argued against the fact that it may
scare clients away, with the words, they are not children. So, glinting on
the utmost platter sat the implement used to castrate cows. They won't
know he had insisted. Kate knew better. Sitting one shelf below, the glass
cylinder sat. Shining. Its contents suggested an other-worldliness. Perhaps
grains from the moon. The jar illuminated the wood on which it sat.
Everyone commented on it. Surely it is lit, by some sort of internal light
perhaps? Kate usually nodded, and mentioned Ikea, uplifters and back-
shelf bulbs. The subject never went as high as castration and for that, Kate
was grateful.
        The gentleman sat upright on the plastic, white chair. He looked
old-school. Kate's fingers rolled down his black, woolen sock, exposing his
ankle. His foot sat naked on her thigh. It reminded Eric of the war. Of
luxury, where silk would be rolled down from upper thigh to pool around
splayed feet. Her hand felt nice. Un-doctor like. The white coat had bristled
with crispness when she had bent down to tend to his foot. And he could
see the beginnings of her breasts through the slit at the top of her coat. A
peep-show of desire. He was enveloped by her perfume. Each way she
turned he could detect the scent. It was a cloud of delight. Moments later
she stood.
        'I have some lotion', she said, 'for this'. Her french was good he
decided. She was accepted here because of her french husband but there
was no doubt that she worked at being french. Eric followed her
movements as as she reached down behind the counter. His eyes strayed
to the cardboard cutout advertisements. Standing either side of the
counter, as if advertising new film releases. Curves of vertical pastel blues
and yellows; perfect countryside backgrounds. Scandinavian healthy
smiles. He belched a little and tasted the liver he had consumed just one
hour before. It made him feel good that he had eaten so well. He hoped
she could not smell what he had tasted.
        'I'll apply this for you now', she said, 'but you must do this yourself
once in the morning and again in the evening'. Returning to his foot, Kate
massaged the white, scented cream all around the base of his ankle. She

rolled his sock back, wincing involuntarily as she touched the short hairs on his leg. Over the moistness. It felt wrong to Eric. Dry over wet.

'I noticed', Eric said, 'the jar. Up there.' Kate followed his gaze. 'What's in it', he asked. Kate's reply was stilted.

'Normally', Kate lied, 'customers ask about the implement above.'

'I understand', Eric replied. 'It holds more interest'.

'The jar, that jar', she faltered, 'it appears to shine. Like the moon.'

'My foot feels better already', Eric said, 'à la prochaine et merci.'

He held her hand in his and looked Kate directly in the eye. 'I hope, one day, we can meet and address each other with honesty'. And as he spoke the words and turned his back to leave the pharmacy, even he doubted if that would ever be the case.

*

They had rejected his previous ideas. A secret brothel. The oldest honey trap of all. His plan to kidnap the government minister's son. They preferred the experiment. They needed 'plants' they had said. People who they could turn to. Who would take orders. Without consequence. Eric ordered another coffee and put on his sunglasses. The early afternoon sun was already seeping through the green cover of the vine. Snapping closed the glasses case he reached into his pocket and opened his notebook. The sun shone brightly onto his scribbled words and initially he had problems making out the feint curls of his letters. Placing the sunglasses to one side he decided to brave the natural glare:

Presumed age: 67. White hair, white beard. Predictable silver-rimmed glasses. Allowed his facial features to blend into the background of his face. Always walked with a bitter briskness. He needed to be at his destination before he left. When he was stopped in the street, as Eric had observed first hand, it was as though a sudden brick wall had appeared. An abrupt stop. A feigned shock at the interruption. Exchanged words would be brisk, un-wasted. Conversation complete he would continue, in his mind the meeting already dismissed. Assumed partially autistic. Useful attributes. Would follow through to the end. Liked authority. Did not suffer what he perceived to be, idiots.

Presumed age: 48. Overly tall, so he stooped. When sat at a cafe, his foot, when crossed, shot out at passersby with subconscious intent. This extenuated his worn black shoes and pathetic dark grey socks that only just covered his ankles. He looked down at everyone and everything and adapted his personality as such. The tip of his dark blue tie was tucked behind the buckle of his shiny belt. It was a uniform of idiocy. He was a medalled general without a war. A retired bank manager without a large, polished desk. He was hanging onto an air of decorum that had been blown away in 2003. Possibly gay. Probably bullied as a child. Exudes an authority that could be exploited.

Presumed age: 36. She was new money. Each day she would paint herself from head to foot. An actress facing the spotlight. Hair scraped back to reveal polished, bright features. Each action was presented with emotion. She would lay her fingers on your arm when emphasizing an incident. Recent occurrences in her life were recounted as stories. A beginning, a traumatic middle and a furrowed brow finish. She surrounded herself with young things. Babies, new Audis, muscled ponies and Belfast sinks. Conversation came easily but never dug further than yesterday. And of course tomorrow. But to dig into that past was dangerous, for Jenny (name overheard in the pharmacy). Too many hidden sticks of dynamite. She has re-invented her past. This can be unturfed. Her lust for money could be used.

Age: undetermined. Always shows too much leg. Hunched in appearance. Could be sciatic . Looks crushed by life. Hair short and blonde (easier to manage Eric imagined). Overly slim. Smokes and drinks (too much). On introductions one assumes Parkinson's' or Bailey's . Carries a searching look as if looking for something lost. Her husband is always present but absent in nature. Her addiction and her lack of goal can be utilized. Shows potential to lie and her personality contains holes that need to be filled. (suicidal potential).

Presumed age: mid-forties - (has 18 year old daughter). Wears hair in bunches (emulation of ever-present youth in her sibling). Infant in posture. One stoops to kiss her hello. Holds a far off stare that never retains a focus. Dresses in grey and black (leggings) and appears asexual at times. Insecure yet proud. Always talks about a recent illness. Probably a secret drinker. Doesn't smile, merely extends mouth into a paper-slit. Hides a mental pain behind a thin, veiled curtain of courtesy. Does not trust outsiders and is happy to discuss why (the war, the economy, customs, drunkenness). Patriotic, almost fascist (but who isn't these days?).

Eric tapped his pen on the notebook. The sun was at full lilt now and he was no longer part of any offered shade. Catching the attention of the young waitress he ordered a water. It was too early for wine and it would smudge his brain. Two small roads led past the cafe, passing either side in the shape of a 'v'. As all of the village offerings sat north of the cafe, Eric was well placed. Everyone who visited the pharmacy parked to the left of the cafe and would walk past where he sat. The french custom of greeting everyone you met meant that he got to know why they were going where they were going. Hands were gripped and pale, paper thin cheeks were kissed. Sympathetic enquiries of health would open up vast waterfalls of information. Had it not been for his training, a single notebook would not have sufficed.

Age: around 30. Stylish in that french way where even wearing a jumper with holes looks good (probably due to the ever-present buttons on the shoulder). Romanesque nose. Hair in a dry quiff. Short in stature but with a strong sense of grounding. Happy overtly. Drinks constantly and not only just where appropriate. Lunch time, afternoon aperitif, evening summer BBQ with friends, last minute invite to the local eaterie. Girlfriend, pregnant and one daughter from a past relationship. Loves children and acts as a surrogate to most of the village offspring. Likes money and while not tight, holds on desperately to it - money provides his tenure in life. Holds back a serious side. When drunk will exclaim his love for everyone. When sober this becomes filtered. He is sharp and likes to impress. Complicit. A good choice.

The television was jammed into the corner of the bar. Its screen was a desert background with a familiar presenter, looking relieved he was still alive. Ticket tape monologue appeared at the foot, from left to right. Eric recalled the wall-to-wall sports of the bars in Boston. Here it was politics. A wallpaper of boredom. Another bland presentation of what you cannot change. A ride you cannot get off. Yet, Eric reminded himself, this was why it worked. After all, one couldn't argue that the public were being fed reduced information. It was all there in front of them. It may as well have been a cookery program. At least the Americans were honest and chose football over reality.

George wasn't religious. He considered himself more a realist. He was someone who recognized the presence of good and evil, yet not within inanimate objects. Within people. He saw the jar as a talisman. Each visitor to the pharmacy was exposed to the jar and its contents and he hoped that in some way the baring of its purity was transmitting a goodness. He lit the cigarette and inhaled the blue, acrid smoke. Smoking in the pharmacy - even after-hours - felt good. The cancerous wisps curling around packets of thrush cream and clouding around shelves of headache tablets. It was a deadly invasion amongst all this clean goodliness. Disease amongst cure.

And George was in control. He twisted the glass lid of the jar and felt the reluctant sucking of air against his pull. At last it was exposed to fresh air. He felt tempted to dip his little finger, to taste a little. He knew it was the evil of temptation and he smiled in its presence. He flicked the finished cigarette into the now cold coffee cup where it hissed for a moment. He replaced the lid and pushed open the shops front door, allowing the alien fumes to escape. As he turned his back to place the jar back on the shelf, he just caught sight of the overly gangly figure of Monsieur Torneau, approaching from the opposite pavement. I'll have to shut the door he thought, otherwise he'll think I have opened. The jar safely back in place he turned to make his way to the front of the shop. Monsieur Torneau was already inside. Pushing the door closed.

Dope, smack, 'H', horse, tar, boy. Eric had armed Peter with what he needed to know. Enough to shoot a warning in front of George's 'close to collapsing' nose. The money was good. It told Peter that this was an unofficial mission and that the infrastructure of village life was at stake. He felt important again, needed. Confiscation became paramount. the goal. He would offer a replica in its place, containing flour. He was being watched, Peter would tell him. Day and night. They had found traces, Peter would continue, in small clear packets outside the village school. Was his wife involved, would be the final question. Peter had left George after that, after he had shown the photographs. The implications were clear. George had agreed to everything. As planned. Eric asked the barman if he could change the TV channel. He was sick of the news. Sport, he replied to the question, anything that is showing sport.

The clear plastic packets, empty and discarded by Eric, had been noticed by Emily as she dropped Sophie off at 8:30 on Friday morning. It was the discussion with someone the evening before, over an aperitif, that had raised her suspicions. She was still shocked to find what had been suggested to be true. She asked Sophie if she knew what the misty plastic bags were as she dangled them in front of her. Sophie was still embarrassed that her mother was picking up litter outside her school. In front of her friends. Emily grabbed the closest parent and begged that they stay with Sophie. Then she ran to the administrator's office, her world crumbling. Change was about to interrupt her gentle routine.

Most addicts - those that are really addicts - will try any new high. Anything that can induce a three to four hour pleasant buzz. Cassie fitted. She was a choice because she was a drinker. And drinking is all about the same thing. Inducing enough alcohol until Cassie was able to face the day. When the hit diminished she had to start again.This meant beginning at breakfast and starting again after lunch. It was cumbersome. The clinking of the empty bottles in her garden shed. The haziness each morning. The parched throat and the gallons of water she had to drink in the middle of the night. The aching of her kidneys. The forgetfulness and the sweats; all forgotten when Cassie was drunk enough. Eric could not act as a pusher. Too obvious. Outside expertise had been called in. The nice guy, in his forties. Gets chatting to Cassie on the Monday evening club night in town. They hit it off. Couple of dances, where Cassie holds onto him for steadiness rather than lust. A kiss in the taxi on the way home. She couldn't believe he lived so close to the school and why, she asked, hadn't she seen him before. Eric had suggested the bus shelter next to the school entrance. She was drunk and open to suggestions. And now her DNA was all over the evidence that was making its way to the administrator's office.

Peter was easy to convince.

"We acted just at the right time," Eric had confirmed.

"I couldn't believe it. Emily told the police what she had found." Eric placed a hand on Peter's shoulder and guided him towards the emptiness of the tennis courts.

"This needs to stay between us Peter, the game has just begun."

"My prints are on that jar I gave you, where that stuff came from.." Eric steered Peter across the road, away from suspicious glances.

"You have to trust that I thoroughly cleaned the jar. It will be examined I am sure by our people and perhaps the police. They will know that you helped me." It was enough to calm Peter for now and also to keep him tagged. "Remember, the rest of the jar will never be distributed. You and I made sure of that." Eric stopped and gripped Peter's hand in his. He shook it twice, looked Peter in the eye, smiled then turned to return to the village. All successful plans Eric decided, depended on paranoia and gullibility.

He could just leave. Abandon the village, after all his job was done. Suspicion had been injected and was flowing through the streets of the village. Distrust bolstered by the bakery, the 'huit à huit', market day on a Sunday. He would only have to step in every now and then, remind people of their roles. They could never walk away. They were his now. His report had been brief but packed with detail. Their answer came back to him as a silence. The highest achievement. He was being trusted to run things. Extra funds had been issued. The jar had been a good choice. Evil was indeed now amongst us.

The pharmacy door swished open at his touch, leaving the briskness of outside where it was, before gently closing behind him. He felt cocooned in this sweet smelling room, full of whiteness and boxed remedies. The small, neatly stacked boxes made him feel organized. Amongst all this ammunition and weaponry waiting to fight for life. Kate was serving a client so Eric browsed the shop. The shelves had gone he noticed, plaster had been used to fill exposed holes in the wall. Perhaps they had been pulled down in rage. Had his replica jar smashed, flour coating the floor where he now stood? The shop appeared normal now with no conversational entities. All talk remained medicinal. He watched the elderly woman leave, slowly but with intent. Eager no doubt to return home and self medicate. Become well again, claw her way through old age. Kate looked up and was unable to disguise a look of distaste on recognizing his hunched form. She looked towards the door, willing another customer to interrupt this virgin silence. A silence that was talking to Kate, telling her why he was here, what he was going to do. Hadn't she promised George? That they would get through this, get past it. Time would help them. Yet she understood why he was standing before her now. I hope we can be honest with one another, he had said. And now she was being honest, to herself.

'It's my leg again, my foot. The lotion worked but I thought - hoped, that you had something else.' Hs tone was confident, assured. He looked around for the white, plastic chair. 'I would need to sit you see, like before.' Again from her, silence. He stared intently at her white coat, looking for fissures, gaps, stolen glimpses of flesh. At last she spoke.

'You had better come through.'

Socrates

by Ian Phillips

The brightness of the sun surprised and flooded their vision as they left the house. As if they were discovering an exit from a dark, cavernous room. Dueting in time, hands went up to provide human shade from the glare and sunglasses were fumbled for.

      'It's a lovely day,' Chrissy said.

      'Blue but fair,' David replied.

Chrissy paused at the view flowing away from the front door. The green undulations dipped suddenly before taking a run up to the hill at the foot of the field. Beyond that she would be guessing. Turning left David started to lead the way, walking in the middle of the single lane that lead up to the main road.

      'This path is like an artery,' Chrissy breathed heavily as she caught David up, 'and I'm not sure what organ our house represents but it is connected to that main vein up there.'

      'And what are we, the filters? Keeping the grass short, the beds free of weeds.'

Chrissy laughed.

      'I guess so. Although some filters appear to do more work than others.'

Walking slightly uphill, the horizon shifted slightly. The aromas altered as they left what they knew and entered the arena of the neighbour's livestock. Of removed crops. The still bruised building that Patrice was renovating held its form yet had changed little in over five years. As they passed the crumbled surface of the driveway that fed away from the lane it held an air of abandonment still. Chrissy said it was too large to fill with total warmth and love. It takes decades to fill a home with love David had replied and Patrice was not overflowing in that department. They both purged ahead, away from a problem that was not theirs to resolve, almost at the top of the road now. Towards the junction.

      It felt like they had reached the top of a mountain. The surrounding flatness meant they could see for miles. All topped with a searing blue. Colours were everywhere and autumn was standing proud amongst the debris of summer. Purple stems lay dead amongst once proud bursts of sunflower. Distant rebellious fields still showed scattered orange where famers were late to harvest. It felt like a decree David had remarked. Leave some colour for the tourists. As they turned left towards the village, in the distance they could see the local's gardens were pushing nurtured reds and fading pinks. And the now empty holiday homes, the golden stone still reflecting laughter and warmth of nine solid summer weeks of intensity, allowed superior weeds of glowing quality to show. These gîtes overflow with temporary love, Chrissy mentioned. Each week overlapping into the next. Where families, thrust together are shown the light of how it is meant to be. But never can, David had reminded her.

'Just stand here for a minute.'

Chrissy stopped.

'It's that time of day. The retreat I call it. When everyone is home from work. No cars are around. Even the birds are resting. The sun is giving it one last go. Like a dying firework. That's why we see all those oranges and reds. Look, it's the the death of a day. I almost expect to hear a "phut".'

Chrissy took a deep breath.

'I know what you mean. It's that cycle. We are within these laws of nature and have no control, you know, of night and day. We just have to accept the light and the dark.'

David grabbed Chrissy's gloved hand as they continued to walk towards the village.

'You know, sometimes I feel it is just you and me in this world. Not against the world but part of the flow. Every now and then we hit some rapids get caught up for a while. Then we are off again. But I never feel like we are stuck behind a dam you know?'
Chrissy laughed.

'I aways had you down for a beaver. Gnawing through whatever life throws in our way. Freeing us up. That's what brought us here. To this.'
The silence interrupted Chrissy and they scanned the same 180 degree horizon for a moment. The air hung with them. Vacuum-like and weightless. And for a while the only movement was the cattle returning to be fed. Their top heavy moldings gliding along the horizon. Silent, slow and uninhibited.

The walk up to the village looked shorter than it was. By foot it seemed about a mile but the reality was a quarter of that. Chrissy's stride always started with a zest and ended with a lazy stroll - arriving within the invisible boundary of centered life. As they walked, hand in hand, David scanned what lay ahead. There was the half built mini-house - as they called it - planted on the very edge of the horizon. Large enough for surely only one person. The surrounding fields echoed its smallness, underlining its inferiority. Yet it stood loud and proud as Chrissy put it, shouting its presence like an unnoticed backing singer in a band. Closer to them now were two holiday homes, opposite each other. They were nice both David and Chrissy had decided. Well kept and loved. And filled with loving people. This affects a home they had agreed. Nurture a home and live in it. Dent the walls with your presence, leave your loving imprints in the plaster - remind yourself that you were here. The last point David had made after a rapturous party one evening but it had resonated within Chrissy. The next building was not inhabited. Make a nice conversion one day. Another 'Patrice' David had remarked in response. A white van appeared in front of this make-shift storage building occasionally causing Chrissy to question if someone was there, living rough but David would not allow this 'wrongness', this element of misfortune to enter his ideal of where they were living.

'He's added a few rooms to the rear, I can see a gas cooker,' she joked. David replied as he always did,

'There's no one living there Chrissy, just the bears.'

The french sign announced their arrival into the village. Signs always stand back a little from the reality, the stonework of what is really the village David had remarked. Chrissy saw it as a declaration. Allowing the reader of the sign to absorb the vision of the village. Taking it all in as a whole. Because once there, within its throng, its beauty, one loses the sense of expectation. The sign gives us that time. The peace was interrupted not by the barking but as David put it, by that incessant yapping as they tried to walk quietly past the slightly run-down home that sat just on the immediate interior of the village.

'It's incredible, look,' David nodded towards the ground floor living room that faced the road, 'they have given the whole room up to that dog. It's the size of a horse. It probably tells them what to do and when to piss in the garden'. A dark figure was visible upstairs watching television.

'They've turned the house upside down,' David continued, 'to please the dog.'

'Perhaps they're Scandinavian,' Chrissy added, pulling David towards the centre of the road and away from the focus of the house. David smiled and absorbed the view on the opposite side of the road, where an ancient orchard sat, its branches dark green and spindly, like an old woman's hands.

'The trees fool everyone,' David said, 'they give all they can to their fruit, then appear to die. Only to be reborn even stronger next year.'

'I hope that's what happens to us,' Chrissy replied.

'What, just to us? It's a little selfish. A bit like Solipsism but you're recognizing there's someone else in the game.'

'I think', Chrissy said, 'that we all probably secretly think deep down that there is only us. In the game. It's how we're built. How we are unable to truly know what another is thinking, only what we know.'

'Or we think we know', David interjected.

'Of course', Chrissy sarcastically replied, 'it could all be a big trick. The largest joke ever played. We're not really here. Or we're all living on a planet the size of a ball bearing that is sitting inside someone's pen.'

'What sort of pen?' David said. Chrissy didn't answer.

David pushed again,

'Of course you wouldn't be expected to answer that question unless you believed in some sort of dual solipsism. Otherwise, if it was just you, making this whole scenario up within your own consciousness, my question just wouldn't matter. I would only be here for your entertainment so to speak.'

'David, let's just walk and take advantage of this beautiful evening. Relish all that 'is'. Now. I'm holding your hand, you are here, with me. That is enough. For me anyway.' David squeezed her hand in reply and they walked on.

They approached Monsieur Totle's house that set sentry-like on the corner of the crossroads. The roads led away from the carrefour like an exploding star, each disappearing towards a distant horizon. Monsieur Totle's house still displayed the battered white, iron chair where he would sit most days. Watching the infrequent traffic. Waving at the passing schoolchildren. Biding his time.

'It's sad he's not here any more', Chrissy said, 'I can still see him in that chair. Just waiting.'

'Your mind fills in the gaps of what used to be. Maybe that's why we think we see ghosts. I like the way his front garden is kept so neat. That his life has not been swept away. They're allowing his house to grieve his parting'.

Chrissy stopped and sat on his wall for a moment.

'I just wish they could leave the shutters open, let some light back into the house. Closing them is sad. Like shutting up the house at the end of summer. The seasons end.'

David took Chrissy's hand and pulled her to her feet.

'Come on you. Not far to go now'.

Reluctantly Chrissy allowed herself to be pulled away from the atmosphere that circled the house, breathing in fresh air she closed her eyes briefly, cementing an emotion within her heart. She wanted to store something about Monsieur Totle within her. That simple happiness where he had just observed what was around him. What passed his house every day. The way he acknowledged the goings on without interference. As if he was coming to terms with his limitations on this life.

A car approached at speed. As always and by habit Chrissy slipped behind David into a single file. The battered Renault thundered past, seemingly oblivious to their presence at the roadside. The air was sucked away from around them, replaced by a calmer, yet still resonating breeze that soon settled.

'Do they understand the 50 km speed limit?'

'They understand they have finished doing something and now they need to be somewhere else', David replied, 'it's always the same, foot down and stare straight ahead.'

'I don't get it. France seems to be pools of tranquility linked by speeding grandmothers. Perhaps it aids longevity. Keeps the old heart pumping faster.'

Chrissy rejoined David's side. Finally the church loomed ahead. Her hand squeezed Davids again. The steeple stood out now. Spearing the remnants of the late afternoon sky. It held no artistic quality, it was just there Chrissy had remarked, pointing up, a useless piece of metal welded to the church roof.

'They're supposed to be divine, steeples,' David attempted to pick up an old conversation, 'literally pointing heavenwards'.

'It's ghoulish and man-made. A gothic finger reaching out and pointing out the obvious'.

'And havens for pigeons apparently. Many Romanian churches have lost whole structures to the rotting feces of these flying rodents. '

Chrissy sighed.

'And hence?'

'All that fuss last year when they were taking pot shots at the steeple. That was to cull the pigeons.'

'It looked amateurish and it scared the hell out of Jeremy.. What about ricochets?'

'You became Linda McCartney.'

Chrissy smiled and pulled David closer as they continued to walk.

'Jeremy was scared.'

'I know.'

Approaching the gothic entrance of the church they both paused and stared at the ancient, cavernous porch empowered by vast shoulders of stone. Someone had scratched in some graffiti into one of the pillars; a wobbly CND symbol and the word 'tue' underneath. The gates that led into the graveyard were new. Heavy, black and designed to keep animals out. One however had swung open. Taking Christie's hand again David gently steered her towards the opening. The graves themselves were an explosion of colour. Flowers burned with oranges and blues and yellows at the foot of polished granite headstones. The plots were vast in some cases as whole families were buried together. Yet each grave proudly displayed fresh flowers. Chrissie stopped, as she usually did, at one particular grave. A young girl who had died at the age of 10 back in 1985.

'She would have been my age now you know.'

David nodded without comment.

'The photograph on her gravestone almost suggests what she would have looked like as an older woman. It's strange, like Dorian Gray.'

Jeremy was lying at the foot of a pine tree. One half of the tree had been sheared naked to stop falling debris covering the grave. The other half of the tree bushed healthily outwards, overhanging outside of the graveyard. Everything within the graveyard boundary was dead, David noted. Even the cut flowers at the grave sides were on limited time. Christie knelt down and plumped up the gladiolas and carnations that she had left a few days ago. Someone had told her that gladiola represent strength of character and she wanted Jeremy to have that link. She hoped that the young girl would be able to help him somehow, both being similar ages. That if there was a place they went, to understand why they had been taken, that someone would be there for Jeremy. She didn't discuss this with David as they had different ways of dealing with grief. And this was her way. She didn't understand David's way, it was more of a robust stance. A 'we can get through this' kind of thing. She only understood that there was no getting through this. There was a kind of limbo, yes, a period of deep, deep sadness and after that it was dealing with the loss on a day to day basis.

David was standing by the tree, feeling the rough silver bark, running his fingers over the notches where the greenness used to be.

'It's good that they think of things like this. I don't want to think of Jeremy under a blanket of pine.' Chrissie looked across at David.

'I dunno. I think it's kind of comforting. Like a nature's duvet. It makes me think that he would be warm at least.'

'I prefer to think that he has gone from here. I hate the thought of him being alone.'

'I know you do.' Chrissie placed her arm around David's waist, 'I know you do.'

Clicking the heavy gate shut behind them they retraced their steps, silence being their partner now as they aimed back towards home. They walked with the church behind them now, past the row of terraced stone-fronted houses that before had held an air of secrecy. It felt now that Chrissy knew every stone, every shutter. Knowledge had been thrust upon her and it sat heavily in one corner of her mind. Another car approached, from behind this time. As it burst past them, Chrissy and David were woken from their hypnotic state and they became concerned for the others safety.

David's hand sat lightly at the small of Chrissy's back and she gripped his hand tightly.

'Look,' Chrissy said, breaking the spell, 'there's two deer, in the field by the small house.'

David looked over to where Chrissy was pointing.

'Three, I think, no four. It must be a family.'

"I never tire of watching deer,' Chrissy continued, 'their presence is so delicate. So temporary. I feel I have to drink up each moment they are here.'

Something startled one of the adult deer and after a brief glance up, they were all gone.

'And there they all go. As quickly as they arrived,' Chrissy, head down, started to walk again, 'such a brief beauty.'

Just after the garden with the white chair, the temperature seemed to change and the fields to their left and right became more obvious somehow. The perspective had changed and the surrounding view was more open. David felt the fields sweeping away from them on either side of the road. Like vast wide green and brown highways, disappearing towards infinite horizons. He pulled Chrissy closer to him as sudden gusts of wind enhanced the encompassing cold.

'The sun will be gone soon,' David said, 'almost time to start a fire. Get out of this cold.'

In the distance their house slowly came into view. It stood solid, as a marker for where they were going. In the surrounding fields the telegraph poles stood linked by forgotten cobwebs of cable, haphazardly connecting each plot of land to the other. As they turned right and started to walk down the lane that would lead them back to their door, the wind settled a little and once again they were cocooned by the gentle undulations of the green and yellow land. Protected from what lay there yet also connected to everything that lay there. David and Chrissy closed the door behind them and shuffled off cold outdoor coats, relishing the new warmth and imbued with the new strengths that the day had offered up to them. The dusk-strewn colours from the fields and darkening skies streamed through the living room windows, encasing the house with a pale glow. Little by little, as they moved from room to room, lights were switched on and fires were lit and another day became replaced by night, nature waiting to be reborn.

Becoming Alice....

by Ian Phillips

Looking back everything seemed so full of colour in those days. My memory holds pictures and cine film that feels slightly over coloured; like a fifties projector, clicking away, showing everyone suntanned and smiling and walking too quickly. I was ten years old and used to spending long, balmy summer days in our vast garden. Green and lush it was bordered by audiences of rose bushes and held a slope that lead down to a scattering of apple and cherry trees. The top garden was rectangular in shape and I had mastered flying my elastic-powered balsa plane around its perimeter, having adjusted various rubber weights, and this made the garden mine. During play time, it was my air space. I owned it. It was however, a lonely garden. My school friends lived too far away. Or had parents who were threatened by such a large house and didn't need reminding. As such I spent a lot of time alone there. Kicking footballs, firing planes from catapults, forcing Action Men to take on ridiculously surreal tasks, that generally involved hiding a lot amongst overbearing musky rose petals and being flung from one end of the garden to another.

The Mol family moved into the house across from our fence towards the end of summer. Their property was connected to ours via two fence panels that sat at the bottom of their garden and linked weakly into ours at the top left, just beyond our bonfire patch. They weren't easy to ignore as an American family. Their two young sons were energy-filled and held that brother to brother relationship that constantly bordered on sibling violence. I would always hear the two of them, usually on a Saturday morning, shouting or laughing. Initially, I spied on John, the youngest, through a mottled hole in the fence. I found his accent enticing, different and vibrant. His voice had a deep resonance and when he laughed or shouted, he meant it. Pretty soon the noises I was making on my approach to the fence were picked up on and I became the one who was being spied upon, this time by heads poking over the top . Once we had worked out that we were roughly the same age, introductions were made and soon I entered the alien existence that was their garden.

It was like going through the looking glass. Once I jumped down onto their side of the fence all sight of my garden disappeared and as such, so did my traumatic memory of what I had left behind. I landed in a deeply shaded leaf strewn circle that was about ten feet in diameter. Above me stood a tree that had been there forever and whose branches were so thick they resembled muscles, reaching out as if in defiance of nature. A swinging rope thicker than my arm dangled above me and as I learned later was set at the perfect height to swing in a perfect loop just shy of the fence and on return swing it barely grazed the majestic trunk of the tree. I would get to know this part of the garden well as from the tree, whose branches aided my climb over the fence, the garden path swerved up towards moss-covered steps that lead to a flatter lawned upper garden and where, just beyond, sat a patio.

As months passed, the more I explored the Mol's house, the more I realised that this was actually America. This house, this garden, this double garage. If I shut everything out that stood outside of this house and garden, if I made it disappear, I could be in America. Somewhere very far away. It was an easy feat. There was a proper basketball hoop. Several real, hard, dimly orange basketballs lay discarded against the garage door. Their fridge brimmed with real American food, bought at the local US army base. There were brands I had never heard of yet who cried out in a colourful and brash way to be eaten. They had turned their loft into an American basement, full of wooden boxes holding toys, books and comics. It smelt of wood and the exposed light bulbs added to its rawness. It made sense to me. A basement in the roof; America within England. A world turned upside down.

Jumping back into my garden it became obvious how bland it all was. This oblong of grass with borders of roses that did nothing for me but puncture my footballs. This garden where friends rarely came. The house and the garden were missing something. They were growing lopsided; everything had a slightly neglected feel. I could see that now. The summer days were just long. They had been balmy and promising a few years ago but now they just hung there, waiting. Inside our house, rooms stood quietly, father-less; abandoned in a hurry. And in the evenings sobs could be heard coming from the living room, replacing the chimes of 'News at Ten' and we would retreat to our bedrooms, waiting for the next school day.

There was another friend that I visited whose house also involved me entering via a fence at the back of their garden. This was the perfect house in my mind. Their kitchen was always warm due to a steaming aga and you could smell Earl Grey tea and homemade bread in every room. There was always fresh honey and fresh porridge. Freshly picked heather sat strewn in hand-made green, stained pots. My friend's family always seemed happy and for them the days offered something. Not just something to get through or get out of the way. They had the best toys, a table tennis table, a room with a piano, a room with a TV and comfortable sofas, they had proper bedrooms where the parents had decorated walls with informative posters about space exploration and evolution. It was Moores's utopian house. I recall once that we were staying there for a few days, I think due to my parent's divorce finally going through. It was my friend's birthday yet his mother went to the trouble of buying me a present – a 'happy un-birthday present' she called it. It was that kind of family. Perfect.

Soon my weekend trips over the fence to America progressed and I started to visit the local US army base, eventually joining the American scouts. Here, as a token English kid, I worked hard at obtaining scout badges and it was not long before my shirt was adorned by small silver intricate emblems. A bicycle, a garden spade, a swimmer. I loved the reward factor. I loved that I was accepted into this essentially foreign environment. I never wanted to go back. Yet each Wednesday, after another scout evening I would be dropped off at my front door and I would re-enter my non-wonderland. And the fence would be sitting there enticingly, reminding me of what was on the other side. And here I was left with deserted iconic reminders of divorce. An abandoned lawn mower. Beatles albums, both red and blue, carrying photographs of the band members peering down at me. A recently installed silver gas fire, now served only to warm eyes that shed tears nightly. A black leather chair, that once swivelled, a child on either arm, the centrifugal force of a father in-between, now sat ornamental in the corner.

Everything had stopped. The merry-go round had stalled and we examining still objects that had once danced on their own. I could not see a way of getting it all moving again. Our sails were too damaged.

As happens with lives that have direction, the Mol's eventually returned to America. The rope was removed from the tree and the new owners of Little America put up new fence panels to replace the old. There was no longer any way to see through to the other garden. And climbing over the fence became impossible as the trees once helpful limbs were pruned back. The door had finally slammed shut. It was time to move on, like it or not. And move on I did. I started to use the lawnmower; I was now old enough to understand how it worked. I started to play those Beatles albums and to appreciate the surreal quality of the covers. The songs served as an apprenticeship to my future musical taste. The black chair in the corner became somewhere just for me to sit. And I kissed my first girlfriend in this chair, spinning it quietly towards the wall, allowing us momentary privacy. And that ghost of myself, my sister and my father, all those years ago, sitting together watching Doctor Who, evaporated into another memory. He was no longer standing in my way. The house was adjusting to his absence. And that time-warp that had allowed me to slip into that other dimension of the New World for a while had now sealed. Its residents were long gone, as if their work here, at the end of my garden, was done.

Killing The President

by Ian Phillips

The boat swayed and the salt hung in the air. Paul sat back and tasted the atmosphere. The plastic seat cut into his back and he observed the excited tourists - excited by what they didn't know. Milling from middle deck to upper, watching only the sea and the foreign horizon.

Did they expect dolphins perhaps? Or exalted waves caused by unsighted torrents or promised sightings of feeding shoals of whales - of which type the clutched leaflets would foretell.

These were city folk mostly, instant experts on the sea. Clothed in yellow-coated rubber jackets that said -'I could sail this baby if I wanted'. They grouped together like quiet Americans, silent in their false, accumulated knowledge. While we, the other tourists, watched and learned. Secretly glad that someone was aboard who knew. And the far off land grew closer and closer.

Paul assumed that he was alone in knowing what he did. It was natural after all. The gently undulating boat rocked along with his secret and he knew it was safe. To his left in the symmetrical block of four seats, two couples sat, one with her legs stretched across her new boyfriend's lap. The other couple, friends of those behind, laughed forward and tossed their heads upwards allowing the sound to travel to the seats before them. Each wanting the others to know their intimacy. It was love's game. And Paul, knowing nothing of this quadruple friendship suddenly knew everything. The signs were too obvious. Niceness bred visibility.

An excited gentleman invaded his space in front, joining who Paul assumed were his two middle-aged daughters. A can of Amstel light was gripped in one hand. Paul flinched slightly as his knee was touched by an elbow as the man flexed the plastic chair and leant back to expand on his two-minute tale.

'There's a guy, upstairs' - he was out of breath - 'he had a set of bag-pipes...'

He was after an audience.

Paul sighed, not certain if it was the story or the invasion of his space he was more concerned with.

He switched off. Or away.

He watched the man gesturing with his removed tartan cap – and he tuned himself back towards the sounds of brushing waves.

The sound was turned low.

As the boat turned towards dock, the harbour responded as if sending sound waves back and it bucked gently, riding over each message with ease. as if to say, Okay, I can handle it, - thanks anyway.

The horn sounded, as it always did and responsible parents covered their young children's ears while more erstwhile front-dwelling pioneers braved the rails at the front and waved towards waiting passengers.

Paul felt his breath grow shallow as he realised soon he would be called for, and he gripped his shoulder bag tightly, as the boat edged away from reckless jet-skiers and sleepy shallow sailors and slowly but inevitably made its way to dock.

Paul knew that he could approach any one of his fellow passengers and enquire of their business and 99% would say, 'Hi, just visiting the sun', or something as banal. He was the other one percent. Or perhaps the point five. He knew that the other point five were staying on the island. What about the guy with the bagpipes? He knew nothing of him. But inside he knew it was the 99% that he really had to worry about. They held a secrecy like him. A front. All had reasons for being here on the island today and like him, not all would hide the truth. Truth had a way of outing itself – like an imposing inevitability. All truth needed was time.

Paul waited patiently behind a queue of about 20 others. Tickets were being handed over to white-T-shirted employees, along with tales of the weather and unnecessary details of where they were staying. Paul just smiled and nodded at the cheery face holding a wad of white receipts, placing his ticket in her out-stretched hand and made his way towards the waiting coaches.

Kaki-shorted guides announced their wares to the approaching hordes.

"4 hour tours of Martha's Vineyard – includes a food-stop. We'll have you back here for the last crossing home. Fares will be taken on board."

Paul was still in 'percentage-mode'.

Sixty percent he reckoned were considering the offer. Chatting to the attendants about prices and routes. And the weather.

Paul joined the other forty percent and milled up the road towards the car and bike rentals.

'Milton's Rentals' he was to look out for. Across the main junction, turn first right and enquire at the main office. The car was reserved in the name of Adams.

The car was brilliantly unassuming. An off-colour white Le Baron. Automatic, of course and as Paul surged off towards the east side of the island, keeping the ocean to his left (as instructed) – he breathed deeply to himself. Allowing a few moments of relief. The blueness of the sea rushed past filling his twenty-twenty vision, yet when he allowed himself to glance towards its intensity – it seemed to pause, as if waiting for a photograph.

The houses he passed were typical Cape Cod. As if the vision of the Cod had over spilled into the sea and walked up the shores of Martha's Vineyard and painted itself anywhere it could.

The houses were quaint enough but extolled a richness. An exclusiveness that allowed only visitors. Stay for a few days but then leave please. Look but don't invade. Paul liked that. It would help in his front of being a stranger. Someone who was naturally inquisitive but who would be expected to smile and move on.

Mrs Wrouton smiled back at Paul.

"We have a special. Two nights, including breakfast. It includes a $10 discount."

"As discussed."

"Right."

Dusk was starting to fall as Paul walked along the sea front.

It all seemed so quiet.

Yet he felt that nature knew what was about to happen.

It always did.

He felt a brisk gust from the ocean and stopped to allow it to envelop his being, breathing deeply.

It was the calm before the storm.

And he suddenly felt tired.

Nature was tuned into souls.

He had read that somewhere, of that he was sure. And as Paul sat up

having being awakened by his five o'clock alarm call he waited for something to happen. Someone to stop him.

Yet all he could hear was the wind in the trees. Nature.

Nothing happens at particular times of the day.

Midnight was one. It all seems to stop then. Pausing for it all.

Catching its breath, then sighing, reminding everyone to sleep.

Six thirty caught Paul strolling away from the guest house, no one aware.

Yet Paul felt awareness all around, as if they knew before the event as indeed they should.

And just for a second he saw the blood and carnage and the aftermath and he turned back to the sea.

Did he see a dolphin or was it a low flying bird, cocking its wing towards him. Warning. Or waning.

There followed a splash and Paul looked up at Johan.

"Six skips."

"The stones aren't as flat here" Paul said ridiculously.

"You would do it?"

"Without doubt."

"Even under threat of death?"

"Yes."

The waves lashed relentlessly ignoring the conversation.

"It may be called off."

"Oh."

Johan spat into his hand and released another stone.

Then Paul saw the dolphin. It glazed the surface, its fin pointing up to the moon.

"The moon still shines without the sun you know."

"You should go home," Johan said, "someone will come."

"And you?"

"Always here. In case."

"They said he'll be gone soon. Someone else, someone better perhaps will take his place."

"And the dead ones?"

"You can't fight what is not here, we can't fight a memory."

Johan flinched. He looked directly at Paul.

"It's what they said about the Jews."

"It's not all about the Jews. There were others."

The stone glanced twice on the surface and sunk. Johan started to walk

back up the shore.

Paul anticipated the crunching sounds and talked in-between.

"You are right and we are all wrong you know."

Johan did not look back.

His arm raised for a moment but just to discard a stone. Then he was gone.

Paul sunk to his knees and allowed his legs to move in front of him. Water spilled about his jeans.

The sun was just showing its face, the moon relenting.

He thought back to the guest house and Mrs Wrougton. The breakfast was tempting.

Another day perhaps.

Plastic Soldier

by Ian Phillips

Location - Motorway, large dark green truck. Going nowhere.

The scuppered green metal flicked dirt from the black boot and the wind breathed air that was too fresh and too cold. It tasted bitter and promised worse to come. But we were men. And men could take the cold. Just as women could take the kitchen Dave had added. Then he had shivered and cupped his hands around that Marlboro Light.

The wind passed away from us, sucking other cars slow enough to care, that had bothered to remain behind us - probably just from curiosity. Staring. Are they going to war?

Have they just come back?

Are they hurt?

A convertible MG sauntered up behind our truck. Hood down. Brave but necessary in this British weather - Take it for what we can, Paul said.

And the MG stared. The driver looked beyond our destination and the woman looked at us.

We looked at the driver.

Lucky bastard we all thought.

And she placed her legs above and either side of the glove compartment and looked over us one by one.

Enjoying every minute Dave said.

And we nodded and watched the driver.

Then it was foot to pedal and he was off - to a hotel, or a restaurant, or the in-laws Dave said.

And we went on.

Location - Winchester.

Winchester is nowhere in my mind and when we arrived it was if that was where we had come to.

For nowhere people.

We offloaded our gear and lay on our beds. Then we thought, collectively. Let's do something.

And the geezer (as Paul had named him) told us - out tonight, but back by 12.

And not too much booze. And we nodded as soldiers do; promising to do more than is ever denied.

Winchester is full of holes Dave said and Paul agreed. Full of holes waiting to be filled. In the streets, in the clubs.

I just saw the clubs as voids but said nothing to Paul, or Dave.

Sad voids. Waiting for people like us.

Location - Club. Shouting above the dim of The Human League.

Want a drink I asked.

No Thanks.

Come here often?

Yeah. It's all there is.

Daylight. Lots of banging and shouting.

Worse than the worse early morning.

When you have slept in and all the alarms in the world are ringing.

Get up.

No.

Not just Get Up.

Get The Fuck Up.

For England.

And we could see the cold through iced up windows

and knew what was coming.

Some didn't get it.

Like, you had to get up.

It'll come, Paul said. With training.

Twatting that's all it is. Don't shave get twatted.

Look cocky get twatted.

Don't play the game get twatted.

I got twatted.

Location - slanting field. Everything is white. It feels different. Not like at school.

Field full of snow.

Just relax and the cold goes.

What?

Sit your fat fucking arse into the snow and think of something else.

But not the cold.

And it goes.

So I did it and Dave and Paul did it.

It didn't work but it's kind of stayed with me ever since.

Just relax, and the cold'll go.

Doesn't work though.

In a room. No furniture. Two fat Welsh gits tell us how it is.

£7 a month for the washing machine. Numbskull 1 says.

What? Paul said.

All the clothes washed numbskull 2 says

£7.

Who dries? Dave said.

You fucking do cunt.

£7 sounds quite good, Paul said.

Sometimes the army gets its man.

Sometimes it gets an arsehole.

We had two of them with us.

Geordie

Geordie loved violence. Loved women - lucky girls.

And loved gobbing, both cheeks gagging, having coughed up

'greenies' so khaki coloured and flavoured that even

General Paton would have applauded.

Geordie looked through you. He summed up your worth to him on a real-time basis. If you were of any use he gave you a minute of his time - he made you want to be useful to him. However pathetic it was.

Perhaps via a joke.

Or a shared experience, an exaggerated story about a fight.

Geordie was going places in his little world.

A world where you could quite easily make out the boundaries.

It all revolved around the army, The Royal Green Jackets. One or two mates, an ex-wife and a son - 'that was gonna be like me'.

And in this little world we admired him.

Because this was where we were at this moment.

And that, Dave said, was what mattered.

Not outside, but in here. Because outside did not exist for us.

Get it on

Covered early-morning hard-ons. Figures crouched over white basins,
washing faces and brushing teeth, spitting loudly.

Conversation is reduced to swearing. Fucking this, I fucking hate that.
Then partially damp jackets are buttoned over roughly ironed shirts and we
are jogging towards the distant noise of diesel trucks and muffled shouts.

One of our crew is already face down in the mud. Easing himself up into a
press-up position, back painfully arched.

When I say, our sado-corporal shouts, no smoking on the parade ground, I
fucking mean it. The sentence is underlined with a kick to the kidneys, just
below the smoker's webbing. He grunts but carries on - pushing and
lowering, sending his mind somewhere else.

Then we are loading our gear into the back of the refrigerated trucks. Our
guns between our legs an extension of our earlier erections. We feel the
grateful warmth of our neighbours and we smoke and watch the
disappearing darkness speed away from us as we head to nowhere.

Square bashing they used to call it. Utter monotony I call it. You need a
lobotomy for this shit.

Around and around, shout, stop, start, stamp and carry on.

Some don't get it. Always the lanky or the short ones.

Here it can go one way or another. If you are really so bad that you embarrass yourself, then you fall on the wrong side of the corporal and you don't come back from there. Throw in a bit of humour, make them laugh at your predicament. Then let him shout at you, berate you - kick you. Face to face. Take it all. Then let him see you trying. Real hard. Let him see the redness in your face, let him see your legs shake. Let him know you are not different, that you can learn to be part of the pack - you just need bending into shape, that's all.

Later, as we sit around doing things to block out the boredom, our corporal pays us a visit. Used to be in Northern Ireland Dave says. Ten years. S'long we all agree. Must fuck your head up Dave says, all that kicking doors down, getting shot at, being hated - then coming here. To train us civvies.

He fucking hates us, I say.

Corporal tells us about the first time he was shot at. You just freeze he says. You don't bother cowering or diving for cover. You hear the whistle of the bullet and you just stop and think - that was nearly me done for. Next time is not so bad. You get used to it and we all nod.

Geordie coughs one up and lets fly out of a window. His mates snigger real time. The corporal smiles at Geordie and leaves. He fucking hates us I repeat.

The Brightness of Snow

The cold is the worst. You can't function properly. Dave got bollocked for wearing army issue gloves. What gives you the right to wear gloves you ponce he is asked. No-one, Dave wisely answers. How the fuck do I clean my gun when I can't feel my fingers Dave later argues. I am too cold to answer and my mind and body needs to be somewhere else. I go to bed at ten. Can't sleep. I sleep with my gun, that manages to hold the cold like no other. It acts as my cold water bottle. You always sleep with your gun we are told. It is your lover and mate. And the army is your mum and dad. All bases are covered then I tell Dave.

At five I am kicked and I struggle out of my soaking sleeping bag.

I can see everything even though it is not yet daylight.

It is time for my watch and I swap one cold tent for a colder outside with a wind blowing that I am not meant to feel. It reminds me of that question - does a falling tree make any noise if no-one is there to hear it? I think so as I am feeling this bitter cold at five in the morning when I should be asleep in a bed, in the warm. Not here. I lie down and take up my position of staring at far off shadows. If anyone approaches I am meant to challenge them - easier to shoot them I muse - and nick their clothes - and make a bonfire out of their bodies. Bones burn slowly I recall having read somewhere. Just as a thirsty man thinks of nothing but a cool drink, I can think of nothing but a warm room, a blazing fire, or a steaming bath. I make a mental note never to take warmth for granted again but I know I will.

Back in our terrapin rooms, warm and dry and well fed, I can think only of getting out of here. Away from Dave and his dry wisdom, that applies only here. That I know would be diluted in the big world. I want all of this to just be memory, an experience that I can look back on - laugh at with friends down the pub who will look at me and say - how could you? And I will shrug and act like it is my dark secret. My hidden SAS.

Passing Out

We are congratulated on a grey afternoon as we 'pass out' on the parade ground. It reminds me of a school playground. Concrete, cracked, bordered by ugly intimidating faceless buildings. These are teachers for grown-ups but they still hold the same bullying traits of the boys you were always scared of but who you watched with awe - hoping that one day you would be them.

My beret is too tight and sends a pain across the top of my head. The speeches are too long yet I manage to somehow feel proud of my achievements, even through the searing pain. When I remove the beret it is as if all the pressure goes with it. We are now free to return home. To civvie street, away from this place of no-return, for me at least.

Home

It feels strange to be back on the streets. To be 'allowed' to go without being told. I think I have just tasted the army and feel that this is what prison must be like and that it wouldn't take long to become conditioned and forget about this other life. It is as if they teach you how to become dependent once more whereas you spend your youth pulling away from this very thing they want you to clutch again. Some call it conditioning yet I call it de-conditioning.

Tomorrow I return to my nine to five job and the skies here remain grey. I still walk amongst darkened streets, tagging along with borderline friends, yet now the fork in the road appears more defined and my choices seem somehow clearer. I can feel the fog beginning to lift.

Autumn's Fall

by Ian Phillips

The phone rang and rang.

Paul knew it would. He listened urging his friend to be home. It was playing a tune that he wanted to hear. Needed to hear. It meant that he didn't have to talk to Suzie. Suzie – all hands-on-hips – screaming-in-his-ear Suzie. It allowed them both respite. He pretended that he had to speak to Martin and she had to stop shouting. Yet she just waited. Knowing that as long as he never spoke, the phone at the other end was never answered. Paul knew it would soon be round two but this tone – this intermittent dull ache that was ringing in his ear – was music compared to that voice.

He hung up.

Bastard's not there – he heard himself saying.

Then he busily began to send a text message. This was desperate yet it worked. Suzie held off. As if his frantic button pressing was a conversation waiting for an answer, 'it would be rude', he could almost hear her thinking. Then there was a pause as he sent the message and waited, expecting an instant response.

Then Suzie continued.

"This can't go on Paul."

It was a terse full-stop to the last two hours of shouting.

It said so much more than the short words allowed,

It said 'we are finished', it said 'let's call it a day', it said 'you win, I can't take any more'.

It said 'Love has died'.

Paul looked up, not at her, but out towards the garden and his mind did a sort of fast forward of them, planting, cutting the grass, building fences – and it seemed like a waste. But a necessary waste. Like the water scooped past by breaststroke in a swimming pool. Necessary in order to go forward. But the structure that he could see in the garden, in the house; the walls they had painted, the curtains they had hung - looked as strong as he felt weak. He was internally damaged. An empty can, rattling and useless. And as men do he wondered about recovery – and towards the next relationship (and towards hers) and he felt a kind of plastic hope that the next woman would really understand him (and that her next man would be a bastard). It raised his spirit and dashed it at the same time.

"I know." He agreed.

He pulled the door shut and looked up at the house as he had done when they had first arrived to view it. He saw the bricks close up and homed in on the one or two crumbling ones and the external sill beneath the window that still needed sanding and repainting. Paul hummed a goodbye and walked away down the path, still not believing that this was it. The end of their chapter, where their lives would actually fork and they would flap their butterfly wings and begin to affect different lives. And it was hard and easy at the same time. His walking away, her staying. Easy to go but hard to leave.

The taxi driver was as cockney and chatty as usual. Full of stories of early retirement and bad driving and always verging on the mildly fascist. It made Paul uneasy. This guy swam in a different sea to him. He splashed and shouted in uncertain waters while Paul put his face in the sea and calmly made for shore. He was glad when they arrived at the airport and he could wrench the door open and expel the car's atmosphere into the fresh air. Tipping the driver, Paul took one of the taxi firm's business cards and mentally trashed it.

"Thanks," he said. But he knew it would not be needed.

The departure lounge was not full. Of course there were plenty of people milling around, standing gormless with trolleys, paid, Paul assumed, to get in the way of arriving, genuine travelers. He had timed it well, arriving after the lunchtime rush, people were on wind-down, beginning to see late afternoon – the end of the day in sight.

"Passport please." And as he went through the checking-in procedure, nodding in the right places, following the pointed finger as his gate-closure time was highlighted, lifting his luggage to be weighed, Paul realised that he had not been thinking of Suzie, until now, and that was a good thing. As he had to move on. To become someone else. The someone that Suzie had really wanted but had not had in him. And he wondered if in this way that by the time he was fifty he would have evolved into some sort of super new man.

"Why can't you be more 'real'" she had said to him once. "You live in your world of offices and trains and taxis – you should see the working man in people. Be more real!" she had shouted.

And in his own way he had understood what she meant because Suzie knew Paul as well as himself. He faltered in the presence of electricians, decorators, gardeners, and plasterers. People who 'do things' Suzie had said. They made him feel superficial and the way that Suzie flirted up to them, asking questions, nodding as another of life's mysteries was answered, reiterating his uneasiness. And now he had made his mind up – he would become more 'handy' in the future. Take courses. Learn. So that when Suzie number two came along he would be that person as well. He would evolve.

Now he was at the gate, handing over his boarding card to be sucked and split by the machine, his £275 original ticket reduced to a slither of cardboard. And he was being smiled at again as he entered the aircraft's tubular environment, queuing, waiting patiently for passengers to hoist heavy bags into overhead lockers, some huffing and puffing, others forcing bodies into 'S' shapes to allow him to pass. Then he was in his seat and he could relax, shut everyone out, stare out through his circular optic as his world became more and more focussed on him.

"Why can't you accept me for who I am? You won't change me. I refuse to change. Not for you."

The last bit had meant to hurt. The first two were slaps to the face. The last was a lunge with a hidden knife. Paul wondered how he had put up with it. But in the final throes of a dying thing it had certain logic about it. Striking out at anything near. And loved ones always stay close by – right to the end.

Different cultures always hit Paul hard. And New York hit harder than most, which is what he needed. Well that was what he had told himself. Go somewhere that buzzes, somewhere to distract and excite. Somewhere to think about starting afresh. A week should be enough. Distance enough to look across the Atlantic and put his small life in perspective. He could think here, think about selling up, and think about decorating a new house. Distance does work, he decided – he just had to make sure he was far enough away to focus clearly. And from here Suzie seemed very, very small.

Paul walked out into the bright, winter sunlight and pushed the Raybans across his view. The exit from the airport never failed to amaze him in its mundanity. You always expected so much yet all that was delivered was a string of yellow and cream taxis. Paul didn't mind. He knew that the real city lay close by – this was just a tender tease of what was to come. You couldn't have it all at once after all.

Little by little, drip by drip. All round him life was showing him the answers, all he had to do was learn how to read. The taxi joined the highway and Paul felt the surge of acceleration forcing him to relax further into the leather seat. Soon the New York skyline would come into view but until then he feasted upon the oranges and yellows of the autumn fall blurring past his window, watching, as shoals of leaves left their branches, making way for new buds. New life. Moving on.

The Theatre of Nightmares.

by Ian Phillips

The aged, dark purple-brown wood of the chairs absorbed any existing joy from the room. They sat skewed. Turned away from the tables. Ignoring their duty. The cash till sat at the end of the bar. A token of modernity, fading green zeros waited to be added to. An aged aroma of already-served coffees hung in the air, reminders of yesterdays. While the silver of the coffee machine didn't reflect much these days, its skin smudged by rushed servings and ignored rub downs. It would come together, it always did. Doors would be opened and customers would trickle in. Full of smiles, false perspectives and poor french. They would carry their dreams on their arms, dreams that were freshly polished and oiled by evenings of log fires and local wine. Chairs would be returned to dutiful positions and tables would fill with batons of bread criss-crossing, their shadows holding baskets of tomatoes, onions and over-priced cheese. The scratched floorboards echoed footsteps like a stage. Minor plays being presented in each corner. Tragedies of health are discussed and actors and actresses frown as expected roles are played out in turn. Beers and coffees are ordered in mirror amounts as men and women play out fantasies of future lives. Expressions can hardly contain the wonderment of what they have discovered. This missing life. Far away from what they know. Men sit contentedly sipping and absorbing the new pub atmosphere. Women chatter and think about nests, the surrounding village offering twigs and worms; suggestions for their new home. And some sit silently, playing out their dreams. Ignoring the hardness of the chairs and the somberness of the empty fireplace. Coffee after beer is consumed. Children are forgotten. Interweaved away from the story. Later to become the final jigsaw piece that would not fit. Hammered into place by demanding fists and raised voices.
       The cafe is almost full. There is only standing room at the bar and the odd chair outside where smokers and realists stand. The chair nearest the door carries the role of chief door-closer. As puffed out and over-coated customers vacate spaces and edge out of the front door, precious warmth escapes. Exaggerated farewells are frowned upon as squeals of see-you-laters are expressed and we all become french within our minds. Within this theatre. With the audience willing you on. Bemused locals watch from the stalls. Glasses of Pernod always half cocked. They hunch together

slapping backs, respecting the distance between them and us. The musty line drawn between those who have the dream and those that want it. Occasionally the line will be crossed and a recent addition to the village will speak in confident tones about a piece of work they need an estimation for. Conversationalists become silent bystanders for a minute then once the deed is complete and the usurper leaves, the hole is sealed once more. And local issues are continued and murmured in low, dialectic tones. Behind the scenes of the arena, backstage - smiles are simple paper-cuts. Performances are ignored and welcomes are fraudulent. Into this place where the dream sits for all to examine, nightmares have started to seep. Once curtains have fallen and another Sunday edges towards the dusk of the afternoon, an extra glass of wine is consumed. To mask the errors of this recital. One that is presented in the same way every week. Confirming insanity while expecting an alternative. As the doors close on the public, shadows fall where once there was light. The empty fireplace blows an occasional cold breath into a room, once consumed by the laughter of unobtainable dreams. Shutters are closed. And a sole lightbulb strains now against the grayness of the afternoon. Looking around at the empty dusty tables, the abandoned chairs - this is the dark side of the dream. This is the side that no one sees. The emptiness. Where happiness does not exist. It is a balance that only just manages to survive. And where one day perhaps the shutters will remain closed.

The Silent Fields

by Ian Phillips

It was the silence that had brought Jessie here. She had been 'carried' here she decided, by the imagery that had been stung into her memory of fifteen years earlier. The flatness that allowed you to see for miles. The square packets of different textured fields with erratically placed horses who appeared content with all that had been placed around them, gently nibbling at the grass while long, healthy tails swished from side to side. Jessie recalled undulating roads that swept through vineyards – around every corner there lays a potential painting her father had said. And now, she realised, he had been right. The taxi swept around bends in the road forcing Jessie to wince at what might be coming at them – the French, her father had said - drive in the shade. Her mother had laughed.

Finally they pulled up outside the terraced stone house. It was close enough to the road to have become part of the road itself. The front door spilled out into potential death. Ones senses would take on a surreal alertness on leaving the front door Jessie imagined. Tuned to the parameters of the surrounding countryside. Recognising the sounds of cars and neighbours' scooters, ready to produce a friendly wave or just to stand and analyse a strangers passing. The taxi pulled up across from Lucy's house in the opposite side track that led to the overbearing church. As a child Jessie had imagined all sorts of evil that lay within this building that presented an overpowering presence over the two adjacent rows of terraced homes. It had always appeared empty to Jessie. As if it had failed to draw in potential sinners so now gazed outwardly, casting a guilty aura onto all who heard its hourly chimes.

Lucy stood in the doorway as Jessie awkwardly handed over cash to the driver. She waved away the change and thanked the driver once more as he placed her luggage to the side of the car. Lucy skipped across the road excitedly rubbing her pastried hands down a weathered pair of jeans.

'Look at me and look at you' she remarked and hugged Jessie closely.

'Always cooking,' Jessie smiled.

'You used to say always homemaking,' Lucy whispered in her friend's ear and she finally held her away at arms length and looked at her intimately.

'I didn't mean...' Jessie began.

'You look happy. Content.' Lucy put her arm around Jessie's shoulder and led her across the road and into her dark and cool living room. The family labrador Honey rubbed gently against Jessie's legs, he had the look of an outside and an inside dog she noted. Happy to lie amongst the stars or at the foot of a bed. Naturally acclimatised.

'Patrick is at work and Amy is at a friend's. Will you have some wine?'

Jessie smiled, paused politely and nodded. She wandered out of the back of the house into the garden that led into a meadow field. She unfolded her arms and sat quietly down on the stone wall that acted as a boundary between the garden and field. The silence was beautiful she immediately decided. The sounds she was used to were jagged and sharp. These were mellow and smooth and interspersed by utter quiet. A quiet that came down on her shoulders like a velvet cloak.

Lucy strode towards where Jessie sat gripping two glasses in one hand and a dark blue carafe in the other.

'I recognise that jug' Jessie remarked, '1987 wasn't it – my last visit here.'

Lucy smiled.

'So tell me. How is life in Richmond without me? Tell me about Paul and work. Is your brother still single?'

Lucy poured the wine allowing large glugs to fill each glass.

'Whoops. Sante my friend.' Lucy raised her glass and handed Jessie hers.

'I'm still single'. Jessie hated that word. It resonated. It underlined her position in life as a loser. An unwanted. 'There was a Paul and now there isn't. I shouldn't have mentioned him in my last letter it was stupid.' - (and desperate she thought). 'Oh, and Jim got married last December, to Trudy. Nice girl. Pretty. Homely.'

'There's that word again Jessie. You used to accuse me of homemaking all the time.' She teased.

'I guess we had other priorities then.'

Jessie shivered. There was a redness to the horizon now and the pastels of the fields were of a deeper shade. She gulped from her glass and sneaked a glance towards Lucy.

'And how about you, Patrick and Amy. La vie est bonne non?'

Lucy still stared ahead.

'I'm sorry we lost touch with each other Jess. I did try and find you you know. After mum died and I came here, I just decided to stay. Life took control of me for a while you know.'

She took Jessie's hand.

'You mum told me about the hospital stuff but by the time I phoned you had checked yourself out. They wouldn't say..'

Her voice trailed off.

They both watched the car in the distance as it appeared slowly on the horizon seemingly cutting through field after field, drawing their senses as it disappeared towards nowhere they knew.

It was like love Jessie decided. Packaged away safely for someone else and moving off at right angles to her life. An unwanted.

Later that afternoon Patrick arrived and the laughing resumed. Lighter memories were recalled and the past fifteen years were mulled over as they poured more wine and picked at fresh pasta. Amy sat on Jessie's knee, while Jessie twirled her long hair into plats.

After Amy had been finally put to bed, Jessie had counted six refusals and two temper tantrums, Patrick made the coffee while Lucy and Jessie slumped into the worn but friendly sofas.

'I love this place,' Jessie thought out loud.

'Careful,' Patrick interjected, 'it's a dangerous and sometimes false love. France holds hidden qualities that aren't always for everyone.'

Lucy pulled a face and grinned at Jessie, 'one quality being that one talks shite after too much wine.'

'No, I mean it. France always clarifies my mind. Helps me to focus', Jessie said. Jessie nodded as Patrick held up the milk carton.

'I love it,' Patrick said laying down the tray of coffee onto the coffee table, 'because it is absolutely not England. That it is indeed Another Country.'

'Where you can hide,' Jessie said.

'Sometimes.' Lucy said distantly.

The following morning Jessie took Lucy's old Renault into the village. On a 'croissant hunt' she had explained to Lucy.

'Two pain a chocolat please' Lucy had called from the bathroom.

'Patrick's at work?' Jessie had asked.

'Yes, dropped Amy off to school – she was so pleased with her plats. Thanks.'

Her words still rang in Jessie's ears as she clicked the front door shut.

For a moment she stopped. Breathed in deeply and continued to the car.

Jessie checked for sudden traffic and crossed the road to the bakers. She breathed in the cool early morning air and marveled at the goodness that had been crammed into the baker's window. The bakers always appeared to her to be the most popular shop and always the smallest. It made her laugh how everyone stopped and chatted within such a confined space and how the door was constantly being opened for you. Here you were met with an immediate 'pardon'.

'I like a good apology before breakfast' she muttered.

Later, seated on Patrick's homemade table and bench in the back garden Jessie was brushing croissant flakes from her clothes and sipping a third cup of coffee.

'Lucy!' Jessie called.

'Hang on' Lucy called from inside the kitchen, 'just sticking one more wash load on..'

'It's just I was thinking back. You know, to when it mattered.'

'Sorry Jess, what was that?' Lucy bounded outside, flushed and holding half a cup of coffee.

'Do you remember Sarindha?'

'From uni? Yes, a nice girl' Lucy replied.

'When she said to us about burning in hell for not covering our bodies to men.'

Lucy laughed. 'Oh my god yes. She said something like – 'I may be hot dressed like this but when you die you will burn in hell for an eternity.'

Jessie looked hard at Lucy.

'I mean, look at all this. All this beauty and we just live our lives and…'

Lucy held up her hand 'Jess, it's a little early for politics..'

'And we just live our lives and allow bad things to happen. Just because it's not in our back yard.'

Lucy sipped her coffee and her eyes smiled at the beauty surrounding them.

She saw beyond the slim white fence that boundaried her garden. Her mind darted with the pairs of swallows that visited every year. She saw recalled days picnicking by the river, laughing at the tourists. Loving the way that she was no longer considered an outsider. It made her feel secure and wanted. She felt contained within this beauty.

'I don't live in that country any more Jess. We both know that.' Lucy paused. 'Have you ever considered why you fell ill? What drove you to it?'

Jessie stroked her forehead and sighed as if recalling a painful memory.

'I know how I feel now,' Jessie said. 'I feel guilty.'

Jessie stood up and paced to the nearby peach tree.

'Because what?' Lucy called after her. 'Because we didn't do enough? Because we didn't save enough people. Enough children. Because I decided to live my life my way? I don't get it Jess.'

Jessie touched one of the already ripe fruits.

'They're still there you know. The memories. Of what we did. People don't forget'. She plucked a peach from the ripest bunch and she held it at arms length, level with her eye. 'When we stopped helping they started dying again.'

Lucy joined Jessie at her side.

'Jess. Listen. Carefully.' She took the peach from Jessie's hand and placed it on the ground. 'You can't compare what those awful people were doing to each other with what I am doing here.'

Jessie kicked the peach. 'All it takes for evil to succeed is for good people to do nothing.'

'So,' Lucy said, 'by me – and Patrick – and Amy – being here. Living and eating and drinking. Here. We are responsible?'

'We all are.' Lucy said quietly, 'in some way.'

Later, when Patrick returned, full of his day and the forced joyful tones of someone wanting to entertain their guest, the afternoon tried to pick itself up. But it never returned to how it was that previous day.

Words had stained the atmosphere and Jessie was now more distant than when she arrived. They talked about Patrick and his plans here and Patrick told Jessie funny stories of distant village cafes and his attempts to cycle home when full of local wine. It was superficial talk, yet light hearted enough to soften things between Jessie and Lucy.

Later that evening, as they sat in front of a pink sunset and listened to the silence they were interrupted by Jessie's mobile. She snatched at her bag and fumbled nervously for her phone. Lucy thought that she looked like she was waiting for someone to call – her demeanor changed. She had become very alert.

'Sorry.' Lucy said and marched off towards the field, beyond the wall, her head cocked to her phone as she searched for a pen and paper.

Patrick looked towards Lucy and raised an eyebrow. Lucy started to clear away the olive bowls, piling up the cheeses on top of the pile of discarded plates. She stopped in front of Patrick,

'She's going tomorrow.' Lucy said softly and started to make her way to the house. The clearing away of food underlining Lucy's end to the evening.

The following morning Lucy knocked lightly at Jessie's bedroom door. She waited a moment then pushed the door open. Jessie was gone.

It was a relief really Lucy decided. The relief when one gets a house back. Back from the grasps of visitors who don't understand personal and homely boundaries. Damp towels could be reclaimed. Two coffee cups now instead of three. Sprawling out on the sofa. And not thinking about feeding other people.

Lucy sighed and relaxed into the cast that was her home. In France.

Patrick appeared at the door to the kitchen.

'She's gone.' Lucy said with a smile.

Patrick's smile did not come.

When Lucy used to watch films – when she lived in England – films where really bad things happened, like, when someone died suddenly. Like a child, or a parent. She used to wish for the ambulance to come and take the body away and for everything to fast forward to five years later. So that she didn't have to sit through all the pain. She wanted to see the grieving partner, or mother, or father when they had recovered. Got over it. Where they were sitting by a lake in a park, reminiscing. Thinking back to better times.

That's what she wanted now. When she knew Amy wasn't coming back. She wanted to be happy again, with Patrick. She wanted another chance. She wanted an Amy and her meadow field. And sunsets. And times when this wasn't true.

She wanted the pain to pass, the hurt to leave.

It was never an accident. She never believed Patrick, she knew that he knew that too. That when he held her, gripped her too tightly – his way of helping her to overcome their pain. It was his way of saying 'I know. I know.'

He understood that the day Jessie had left, she had carried their love away, leaving behind a void.

'It's easy to blame everyone' he had said. And Lucy thought back to the silent way Jessie had left. The phone call. Amy's crumpled body.

Sea of Souls

by Ian Phillips

Tom sniffed the cold, impending breeze. Winter was coming and soon the land would be frozen. His gaze followed the rickety horizon of the garden's boundary and beyond the overgrown track he could make out the silhouette of Émile's farmhouse. He remembered the
fence boundaries needed repairing but the ground was too solid for a pick axe now and the air hung deathly silent as even the insects succumbed to the season's bitter message. Zipping up his jacket against the swirling wind he motioned to Rupert to take the other end of the oak beam and they loaded it noisily into the rear of the rusty, green pickup. The echo rang out into the empty early morning air, bolstered by the firing up of the coughing diesel engine that spewed clouds into the barely-lit frosted morning. Leaving Rupert to finish loading the tools, Tom entered the kitchen through the side door and relishing the wall of warmth, he filled his coffee cup. Hearing the bedroom door slam shut Tom's thoughts returned to Sarah. She would be leaving soon. Checking his watch Tom ran his finger along the crevassed line of his jaw
and sighed, throwing the coffee dregs into the shallows of the kitchen sink. Noticing the coffee-splattered forks and spoons he ran the hot water, watching the swirls of debris disappear. Warmed by the coffee he loosened his jacket and stepped outside, stamping his feet hard on the metal rims of the boot scraper. He imagined Sarah's voice as she watched him, asking him why he hadn't taken his boots off in the first place. As Tom re-entered the warmth, the strong, burnt toffee aroma of the coffee was infused by perfume as Sarah entered the kitchen. Tom was taken aback for an instant by how immaculate she looked, theatrical almost, in her clean, crisp uniform. Next to his ripped, paint-stained jeans and unwashed sweatshirt she became untouchable. Sarah paused in front of the mirror, touching the corner of her mouth while looking directly at herself.
'I have to go,' she said and turned to blow kisses towards Tom. Then amongst her flurry of perfume and thoughts of the day ahead, the front door slammed shut and she was gone. Tom, hearing her car start,

thought how sweet and smooth her engine sounded against the brash chug, chug of his ancient Renault van.

He could have just posted the letter. He could have used the internet at the library. But the village library kept to strange and erratic opening times. And Madame Molière saw any use of the library computer as an intrusion. He felt safer with a box number. It was safe, traditional and respected. It was something you could touch, not physically, but in your mind. Mail was delivered there and you collected the mail from your box number.

'One euro fifteen,' Madame Ganthier had said. Tom had passed the envelope face down but she had turned it over and exposed the address. As he walked away Tom looked up and recognised M. Durand standing next in line. The letter was still in her hand as she served him, a topic of conversation perhaps but Tom could not be sure. He had felt his face redden, the heat of realisation dawning as the tin bell announced his departure.

Each evening just after six, Tom sounded the horn as they arrived at Rupert's house. He was not sure for whose benefit this was for. Whether a warning for Rupert's usually sozzled wife or a way of Tom underlining the end of Rupert's working day. It had become a habit that left them both smirking and Tom liked that. Watching Rupert disappear into the house in his rear-view mirror Tom smiled and driving back towards the village, he turned on the radio. Staying focused on the poorly lit road ahead he patted his crumpled jacket on the passenger seat, searching for his mobile phone. The signal was poor here and he wondered if Sarah had been trying to call him today. Mondays he would usually get a text explaining her lateness. A 'textscuse' he called it. One more house to show, a client's notaire to meet with. We can eat later. Wednesday it was the gym and usually on a Friday there were weekend viewings to plan. No messages today though. Histhoughts darkened as he approached the sepia lights of the village. There had been a shift in attitude towards him. He could feel the village turning. The withering look from M. Vigier when he bought his early-morning criossants. The unnatural silence of the Post Office. The silent nod from Thomas as he replaced the petrol pump where before there had been an ' à bientôt Tom.' Tom parked untidily across the road from the post office, aware that Madame Ganthier closed at six thirty precisely. Reaching for his jacket Tim remembered the scarf in the glove compartment and taking it he wrapped it loosely around his neck. He paused to breathe deeply into the scarf creating a temporary pool of warmth around his mouth and ears and reluctantly opened the car door. As Tom crossed the road the uneven cobbles reaffirmed a feeling of imbalance and uncertainty. Approaching the heavy door Tom pulled the scarf down under his chin and prepared himself for what lay behind the faded, textured windows that, as he got closer, glowed with a dark, golden tinge.

Tom placed one foot gingerly on the travelator and tilting upwards slightly, joined a throng of people all moving at the same pace, all traveling towards the maze of exits that lay below Gare Saint-Jean station. He was encased within a false warmth that would soon be replaced by a combination of the cold, alongside competing coffee smells and hastily, discarded cigarettes. Tom felt more at ease than he originally thought he would. He felt good in his suit and the coat and scarf he had selected did not look or feel out of place as he shuffled alongside the insistent crowds. Shoving his hands into his pockets he braced himself for the ensuing cold as one by one they were presented as deliveries to the catacombs of Bordeaux's under streets. Finding the bar had been straightforward. A stone's throw from exit seven of Saint-Jean she had explained. And as Tom sat waiting, sipping a beer he wondered if he really could throw a stone from here and test her theory? She was beautiful. Even more than her photograph had promised. A vision. A delightful, refreshing vision. Jessie she had introduced herself as, and laughing she had begged him not to call her Jessica. Tom had stored this piece of information hoping that one day 'Jessica' could be used as a play term. I am Tom, he had said. And from that point onwards, introductions complete, they had talked and listened and laughed, the bar noises acting as a perfect backdrop. Jessie's perfume was lighter than Sarah's. Her smile felt like it was meant for him. She was interested in the boundaries of his day. Her conversation linked in with his and her carefully chosen words held a quiet passion for life. When four o'clock arrived and Tom had to go he did not mention that he was going home, only that he had to head back. He hoped that Jessie had noticed. Jessie, attempting to summarise everything that she still wanted Tom to know, nervously explained away the remains of her day and Tom was relieved at how mundane it sounded. He wanted her day to level off when he left. Back on the travelator and heading back into the depths of French Subterrainia, Tom looked around and realised how at ease he felt amongst this crowd of gloomy commuters. His mind flew home and he smiled as he thought of those stray sunflowers that each summer sprung up within the invariable greenness of the cornfields. The seeds blown there by nothing other than fate.

Pushing the front door partially open Tom remembered his mud-caked shoes and stooping to loosen his laces he observed Sarah as she sat at the kitchen table. She was leafing through the local newspaper, one hand curled around a half-empty mug of coffee.

'Oh hi, you're back early.' Tom looked at his watch, no he wasn't. Within the confines of the kitchen they danced around each other, avoiding contact. Tom reached for the kettle then waited as Sarah scrubbed at the sink surround before folding the cloth and laying it by the chopping board. Throwing a teabag into a mug Tom watched as Sarah completed the weekly routine of noisily emptying the contents of the fridge into a half-ripped Tesco's bag. She felt him watching her. 'It's beginning to smell,' she said. Tom's mobile rang and answering it he moved into the living room. It was Rupert.

It felt strange pulling up outside of Rupert's house. The routine of the day had already been completed two hours earlier. The car horn sounding, the see-you-tomorrows, the slam of the door and the spin of the gravel. Tom felt like he was interfering with fate. Rupert was already standing by the front door, still dressed in his overalls. Tom placed his mobile into his inside jacket pocket and taking a deep breath, got out of the van.

Rupert's hand shook as he gulped at the glass of red wine. Tom poured himself a glass and noticed that this was bottle number two for Rupert. The kitchen smelt like the inside of the fridge at home. There were red pasta sauce stains on the oak table along with flickerings of dried, yellow rice dispersed at intervals between where they both sat. Rupert looked a mess.

'Are you sure she has gone?' Tom said.

'A bag is missing. I think most of her clothes are gone'. Tom sat quietly trying to picture the scenario but he knew little about Rupert and Natalie. He grabbed glimpses of her form as he dropped Rupert off in the evening, hunched over this very kitchen table, a half empty bottle of something usually nor far away. Sometimes he received a half wave of acknowledgement but mostly not. He didn't discuss personal things with Rupert. Only factual, must-be-done stuff. Future jobs, costings, VAT, quotes, trade prices. It was more than enough to fill the silent gaps in their day.

'She may have met someone else. Maybe she was bored?' Tom's hand swept around the room, 'of all this.'

The pub had been busy but Tom found a small round table by the window.

'Is Pauillac OK?'

'God yes,' she replied, 'after the day I've had you could leave me the bottle'. Tom removed his coat, he was sweating already. Folding it awkwardly over the back of his chair he sipped his beer and turned back towards Jessie.

'I've made a decision,' he said, 'and I think we'll both need the rest of that bottle.'

Rupert had fallen silent again. The wine now masked any chance of further reasonable conversation and Tom was bored. He understood now the shallowness of Rupert's character. This was all there was to Rupert. No sophistication, no ethos to his life, no culture. Just this house. This table. These stains. Rupert's soul was turned inside out and it revealed nothing new.

'Maybe she felt trapped,' Tom finally offered. 'I mean, look around us, all these open fields, vast blue skies and still our lives are so small and complicated. Maybe we're just not qualified for this simple way of being.' Tom reached for his car keys and paused staring at the view from the kitchen window.

'This was all she had Rupert. You should have seen that'.

Tom found Sarah in the living room, the French news on the television providing a wall of background noise as she scribbled a note in her filofax. She looked up for a moment and conceding to his presence, returned to her notebook. Making his way up the stairs Tom gently closed the bedroom door behind him. From the bedroom window he surveyed all they had built together. If only the inside reflected the beauty of the outside he mused. He pushed the handle of the upper pane and jerked the wooden frame open. He felt the mustiness of the room being replaced by the sober chill of the approaching evening and breathing in, felt at once empowered, his soul feeding on the fresh rush of oxygen. He looked down at the bed he would never sleep in again, at the soon-to-be-empty drawers, at the red case, slotted hastily under the bed that would be filled with shirts, hangers, shoes and handfuls of t-shirts and odd socks. He looked around the room and thought of Sarah. He thought about the fact that she probably knew and that she had really been leaving him for years. At the front door he hesitated, not sure if she could hear him lifting the latch and pulling the door open. The folded note lay under the telephone and glancing back he thought about what he had written and felt a sadness that they could not be spoken words. He recalled that when he had sat down to write the letter, he had been able to visualise Sarah, sitting across the table from him, agreeing with everything he said. Two souls, waiting to be born again.

Another Day.

by Ian Phillips

The beat of the traffic annoyed Peter for some reason. It was in his way. Pausing just outside the Marie's office, he waited impatiently for a gap. The whoosh whoosh of car after car was continuous. Peter settled his anger on each approaching vehicle, hoping that the occupants could feel his frustration. It was as if each passing car was laughing at his inability to cross this river of traffic. Finally, as he glanced to the top of the road where the roundabout filtered the dripping congestion, a pensioner caused a gap by stalling at the junction that lead to the river. Peter bounced across the road enjoying the frustration of the queued drivers and their interrupted flow. He imagined them banging their steering wheels and envying Peter's brief freedom. Stepping out of the well of the road Peter took note of the three offerings that flooded his immediate vision. One offered Chinese food, although not now, it was day time after all. The other simply sold tea. And to his far right stood a bank, closed and mundanely coloured in business greens and blues. Yet money, food or tea was not on his agenda today and Peter strolled up the gentle hill that lead to the church (was this deliberate he thought) - enjoying the crowd-less pathway. He wondered at the stream of traffic and the empty sidewalks - where were these people going? Out of this town he hoped. For a moment Peter paused in his quest and turned back to stare at the river. He could just make out the reflection and the four circles that supported the bridge, feeding the people into the main town. Then the sun hid behind a cloud briefly and the bridge resorted back to simple semi-circles, the reflection melted and the dream was broken. Peter thought about diverting from his chore. He could stroll up the main drag of shop's and take a coffee and simply people-watch. There was Alex, who worked in the 'Orange' shop , whom he could pop in and chat to but this was just after lunch and he knew the shop would be busy. Instead he decided to focus. After all, he had other things to do and Peter momentarily consulted the mental list of jobs he should be ticking off as 'done'. Yet the list melted from his thoughts as the sign sprang into view - 'Coiffeurs' and just below was a union jack sign, A4 sized, onto which was written, 'English spoken'. The whole shop front was tinted glass. Deliberate Peter thought. So you cannot see inside and assess if it is worth waiting. He knew that once he opened the door of the hairdressers and passed into the threshold of enquiry (Can you cut my hair?) that there was never any going back. It was a clever ploy. A template adopted world wide he assumed. If he was honest, the statement of being able to speak english, put him off slightly. Although his french wasn't brilliant he knew he needed all the practice he could get. Already Peter was making up his mind to insist on speaking french, however bad he sounded. Seeing another gap in the stream of traffic, Peter darted back across the road. He planned to walk past the hairdressers from a distance, see if he could see anything within. Something that may put him off from committing. The hairdressers was pushing him away as if it exerted a magnetic field and Peter respected its presence as he strolled on the opposing path, past the glass door, trying to glance into the false darkness. Hoping that a little distance may make the darkness less murky. Just past the hairdressers was a narrow lane and skipping back across the road he turned immediately left back towards 'Vieux Ville' and then stopped. He had seen nothing through the glass. It was no good he was going to have to commit. Peter took a deep breath and started to walk back towards the hairdressers. He was now facing the roundabout. and became mesmerized momentarily watching the unmoving wheel, churning the cars round and round before casting them away in various directions. To Peter it seemed like a machine that never sleeps. The door opened inwards and via a white handle that pushed down like a patio entrance. As Peter was about to walk in another customer was just leaving, stopping to bid the hairdresser farewell once more, such is the custom of parting in France - always overdone. Peter waited patiently, thinking that perhaps she was about to close, that this was her last client of the day. Yet as the doorway emptied and he filled its space, the hairdresser's smile was wide and welcoming. Of course it's not a problem that you have not made an appointment, yes I can cut your hair straight away. Peter relaxed. Their initial communication had been in english. He was determined however to cross over into french. As she guided Peter to the rear of the small shop, away from the three blue, unbarber-like chairs, he enquired in french as to whether she was busy today. Her reply was partly in english and partly in french. It was a promising start. As Peter leant back in the comfort of the leather seat and felt the cold porcelain surround his neck it was countered by the warm water caressing his head. Her hands replaced the thin jets and massaged the shampoo into his hair. Touching below his ears, his temples, as if knowing where he wanted to be touched, sending him into a hypnotic dream. Then it was back to the water, that felt abrupt almost, rinsing away all the good that she had done. And he smiled inwardly as he saw that she was about to apply conditioner, so the process would start again. Peter closed his eyes. He thought she was around thirty. She was very french - in that she was effeminate, dressed unfussily, yet with panache and she held herself in a particular way. She seemed proud. Her manner was confident and as she ushered Peter to one of the blue seats and placed the heavy black mat onto his shoulders to protect his clothing, he noticed that she would glance up every now and then towards passersby. Perhaps in hope of business, he thought. And he wondered about the tinted glass. How it offered a protection of sorts, where she could see everything going on on the street yet she was invisible to them. Having agreed on what length Peter's hair was to retain, the hairdresser interrupted their brief conversations with the buzzing of the hair clippers. It gave them both time to refuel. Flicking the clippers off she remarked on the wedding party that was taking place outside the Marie's offices. Gesturing with the clippers she said in french, another marriage. Peter took up the baton - there are many marriages in France, he rather over-officially replied in his best french. Yes, she replied, but many divorces. The clippers buzzed back into life and Peter clambered for an interesting reply, trying to work out the correct tenses and order of words. He decided to risk talking above the noise. I have been married twenty five years, yet having spoken the words he regretted their supposed hands-on-hips exuberance. I married young he added as an apology. She sparked into life and placed the clippers next to the sink, their use complete. No, she cried out, unbelievable. Then a silence. Scissors were being selected. A glance back towards Peter's hair, then back to the pouch that sat just below the mirror. Peter didn't catch her next remark but it sounded similar to 'well played' or well done. He didn't reply. It sounded like it was a closing statement to the conversation. As she snipped briskly and professionally, she asked Peter about his children. He supplied the information without padding. Ages, education, where they lived. He didn't want to sound like he was reveling. Yet he wasn't sure why. He decided to ask her about her life, her marriage. Any children? All were negative. Even, she replied, the question about her life. I have never married, no there were no children. Just a man. The door squeezed open slowly and the street eased its way back into the hairdressers, invading the silence that they had been sharing. An elderly man bent around the door and enquired about a later reservation. An appointment to help fill his day, where his hair would be trimmed and he could offload to her about the many small issues that intruded and stopped him from enjoying life. Her smile was as broad for this gentleman as it had been for Peter. Not a problem. See you later. Then he was gone and the music of their silence returned. It was a difficult eight years, she continued, quietly and in french. There was a lot of violence. He used to beat me. I became very ill. Then he went to prison. Now I prefer to be alone. I trust only animals. Peter's expression changed and became all the more apparent as they were both staring at his face, she in the reflection of the mirror. That's horrible, he said. Silence. Then he made a quip about how good dogs are as company. The word's felt as if they were taking up oxygen from the silence. Useless. Unnecessary. Yet he wondered how often she raised this with strangers. Did his face fit and offer her emotions somewhere to go? Did he come across as being a listener? Surely all her customers had to listen? Peter studied her form in more detail as she stood up to find a comb. Where before he had seen confidence he now say frailty. Her initial confidence hid a fragile state of mind. And the tinted glass was a necessity not a feature. She needed to see everything that was coming her way from now on. The outside world had become a threat. As they continued to exchange pleasantries - away from the subject of black eyes, bloodied lips and - Peter imagined - broken bones, he really wanted to say something. To leave her with a positive statement. That it really was going to be alright and that there was someone out there. For her. Christ there is for everyone. That she should not give up hope. But even as he was thinking these thoughts, he knew that she had not given up on hope. Hope had given up on her. And that she was going to be alright, just not in a very nice way. Not in the way that Peter wanted her to be. Laughing and sharing a bottle of wine with someone. Looking forward and not constantly back. Her stark reality and understanding of life had been taken from many long years of violence. It had underlined her place in this life and she wasn't taking it any further. She had been told and she had understood. Peter wasn't going to change that in one sentence. As she held up the mirror to show the part of his hair that he could not see, he caught a double reflection of himself in both mirrors. Different perceptions. Different angles. As he stood and thanked her and fumbled for his wallet, she brushed his shoulders, removing evidence of their encounter. It was tender and personal and held together by the vacuum of the shared space. As he slipped a note across to her, she smiled. The door breezed open and there stood the man from earlier, he was predictably early. Eager to begin their appointment. Peter understood that their moment was lost. Any words spoken now would be diluted by the noise from the street, polluted by the cars still rushing by. Taking ownership of the door from the elderly man he stood for a moment in the shop's entrance and watched as she busied herself with her new client. Offering all that he had been offered. And even though the man was not seeing her, only the reflection of himself in the mirror, Peter knew that she preferred it that way. To stand in front of the mirror and not be seen.